SURVIVING BUSINESS SCHOOL

A 'Nikdraws' Collection

Nikita Dawda

An Imprint of

MAPLE PRESS PRIVATE LIMITED
office:A 63, Sector 58, Noida 201 301, U.P., India
phone: +91 120 455 3581, 455 3583
email: info@maplepress.co.in
website: www.maplepress.co.in

Surviving Business School *by* Nikita Dawda

ISBN: 978-81-94845-04-1

10 9 8 7 6 5 4 3 2 1

Cover Design @ Aditi Shah

Dedicated to everyone
who wonders if I'm drawing about them, I am.

Acknowledgement

To be honest, I never imagined I'd end up illustrating a book at Business School. Through the 52 weeks at B-School, I found intellectuals, and I found experts. I found experience, and I found passion. I found talent, and I found sheer grit.

It has been nothing short of humbling. The love and encouragement of my fellow ISBians for 'Nikdraws' kept me going through the ups and downs of the program. I am both grateful and flattered by their enthusiasm for it.

Special thanks to:

My husband, Tarun, who started the 'Nikdraws' page one fine morning and inspired me to pick up illustrating.

My dearest Grandfather, who has earnestly requested for the first copy of this book.

Mum, Dad, Kapil and Pallavi - my biggest source of cheer and strength.

My friends, who helped me merchandise, market and distribute the book at ISB and otherwise - Pai, Anmol, Rishabh, Ahona, Surya, Aakash, Eipsita, Varshney, Priyanka, Rajat, Harshit, Harshita, and Sanchit. Back at ISB, we set up art stalls, gave away freebies, distributed hundreds of souvenir copies - none of it would have been real without their constant help!

My zen-inspiring kitties - Cleo and Kulfi.

Giri, a dear friend I lost, whose passion for life stays with me and pushes me to live large each day. He was one of the first to buy my "autographed" book and told me to never stop drawing! 😊

Till we meet again,

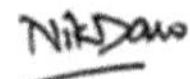

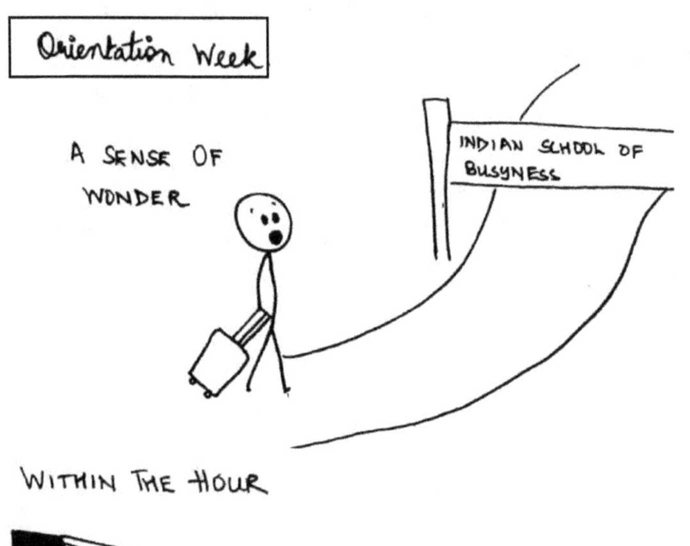

Week One – designed so you can bond with your class mates through "fun" team games.

One way to get over the problems of limited Facebook friends is applying to Bschool.

Remembering Names

Week 1

Spewing 98 names/minute.

The diversity you wanted

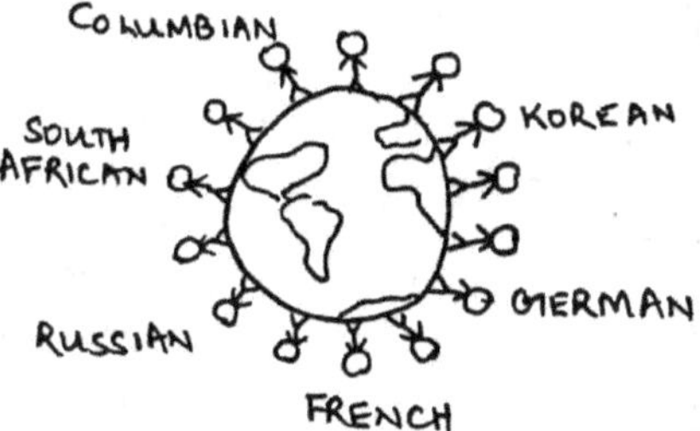

The diversity you got

NikDaw

It's not that bad actually, it's worse.

The Fear of Missing Out is everywhere.

A cute girl you can ask out so all this shit will be worth something

Not supposed to be funny, for a lot of people.

<u>confidence levels</u>

<u>Team 1, Week 1</u>

Two quizzes, one case study, one group assignment, one individual assignment

<u>Team 1, Week 2</u>

Four quizzes, 200 pages of pre-reads, 2 group assignments, 2 study group members on ventilator

NikDaw

Term 1— that crazy wacko, nobody makes friends with.

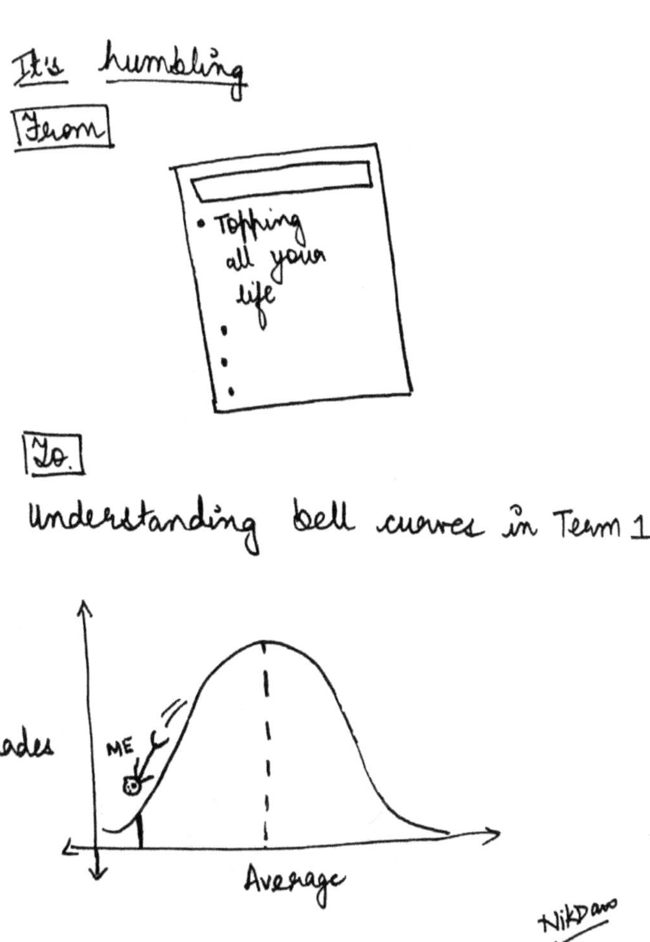

B-school does wonders for your confidence.

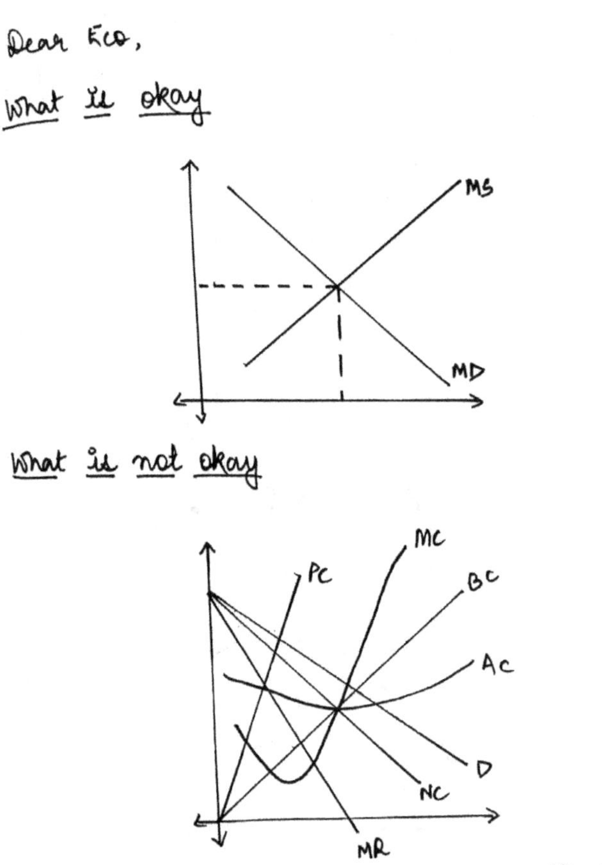

The graph stuff escalates quickly.

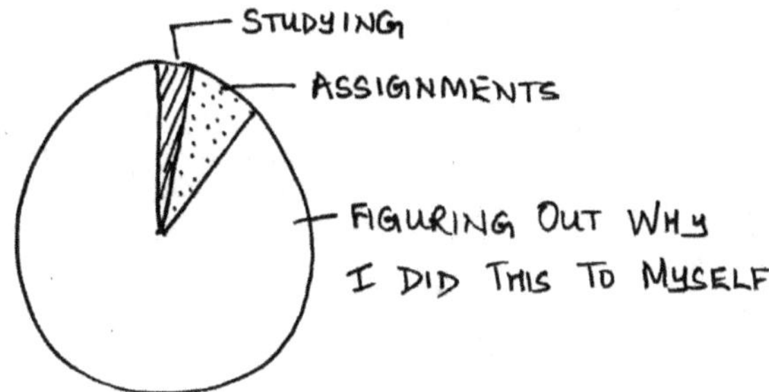

The introspection costs you about Rs. 30 lakhs (non-inflation adjusted).

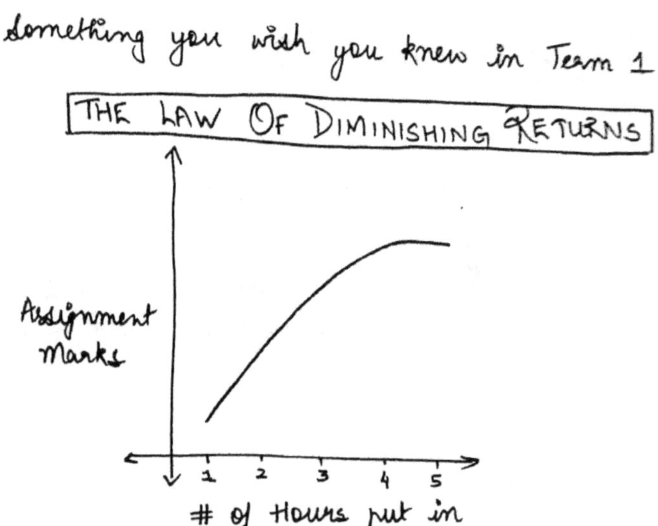

You typically work till your eyes become potatoes.

The first signs of adversity show up in parties.

There are freaks. And then the mother of all freaks.

Nuclear fusion with flat mates as atoms.

leading cause of heart attacks in Term 1

studying normal distribution be like...

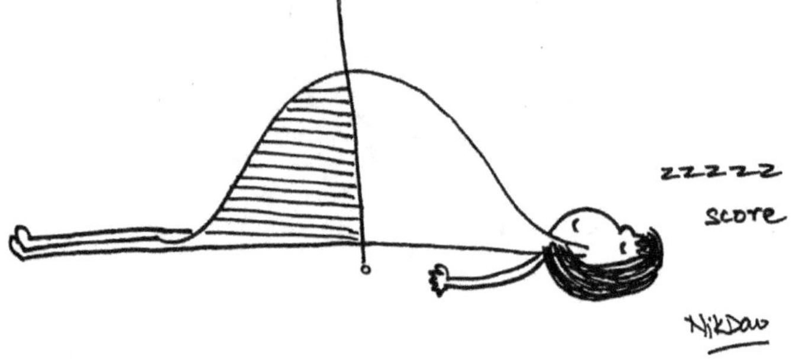

Expectation setting for hostel expenses done right.
Statizzzzztician much?

While discussing weights for
different social media channels...
ACPE: Twitter is the best medium
for celebrity driven fans like
Sephora's.
Prof: So what % of the total
have you given to Twitter?
ACPE: 5%
Prof: Do you have commitment
issues?

Prof talks about how you can
figure out a competitor's
marginal cost...
Prof: (Jokingly) You should
definitely dive in the dumpster
behind your competitor's
office and find their cost
documents.
ACPE: But wouldn't firms
have these documents in
soft copy?

(Class Participation is an important grading
component at B-school).

Every class harbors a handful of "Arbitrary" Class
Participation Enthusiasts dying for points.

Ba(y)es Theorem

$$P\left(\begin{array}{l}\text{finding a}\\ \text{soulmate}\\ \text{at BSchool}\end{array}\middle|\begin{array}{l}\text{you suck at}\\ \text{relationships}\\ \text{generally}\end{array}\right) \approx 0$$

NikDaw

M(BAe).

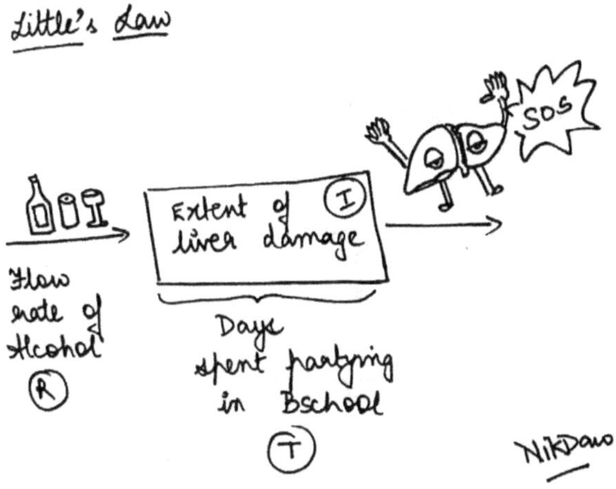

Applying 'Operations Strategy' to everything.

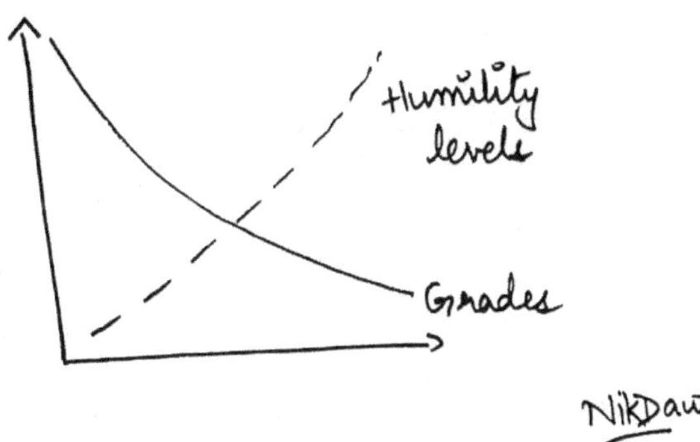

They exist to set academic foundations and murder self-esteem.

(The initial terms are also called 'core terms').

<u>what we're studying</u>

<u>what they're studying</u>

NikDaw

That mass hiss–teria about snake sightings on campus.

When accounting hits engineers like a speedy bus.

case study Readings

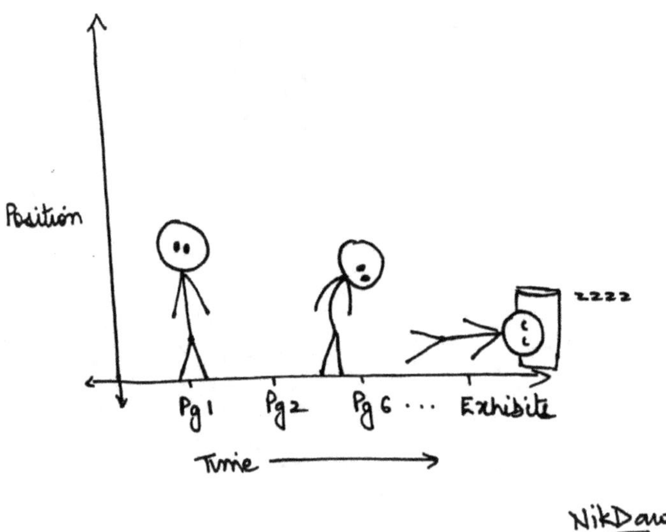

The cure for insomnia, ladies and gentlemen, has been discovered.

NikDaw

*Relationships are fragile. *Pun intended**

Taming a beast called the 'Study Group'.

QUADDIE
(noun)

You'll start making some real friends, along the way.

7.5 MINS LATER

The "delight" of having housekeeping shine your rooms.

How class handouts work

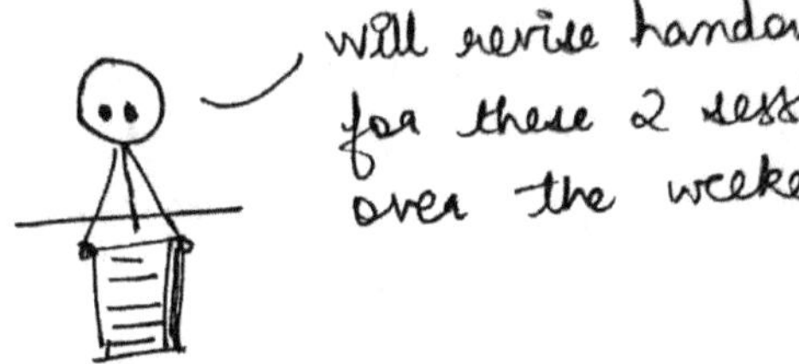

Weekend

Getting up to speed be like.

Survival of the Loudest.

Maslow's Hierarchy takes a twist.

Party's five forces analysis

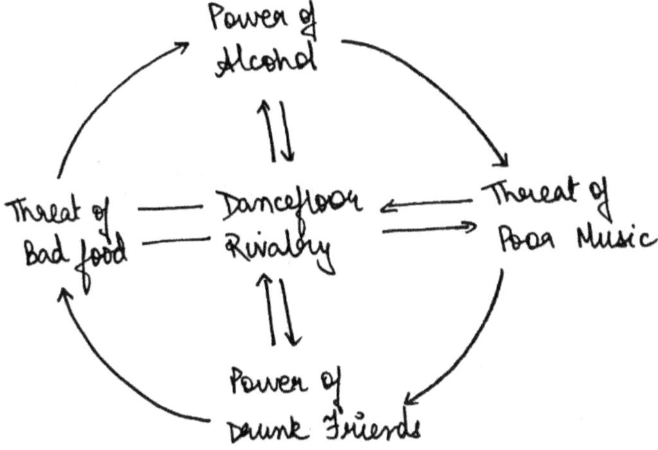

How the attractiveness of a party is established.

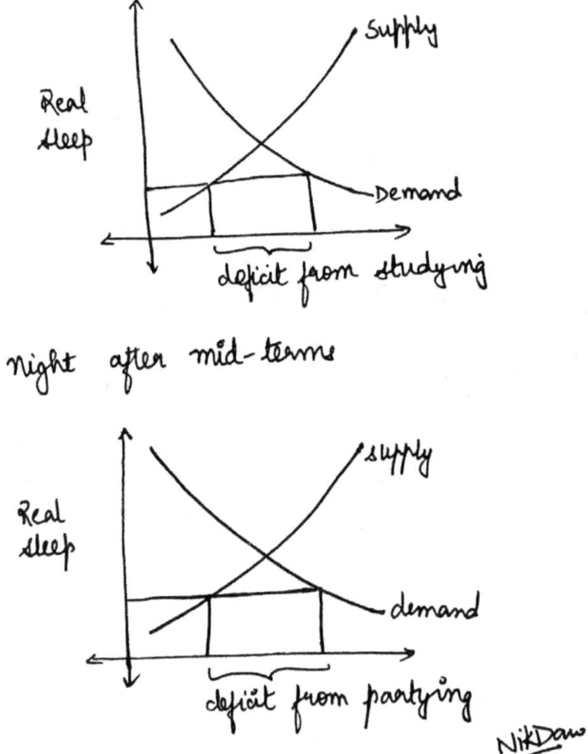

Mid-term exams, an altar for sacrificial offerings of sleep.

We're all 'suckers' for networking.

Murphy's Law

The next class we _all_ read 40 page

NikDaw

The real learning is not in the case, it's in knowing when to read it.

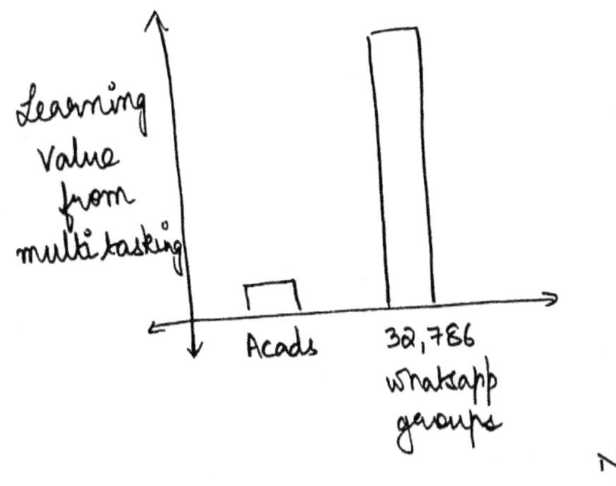

There was once even a whatsapp group for spotting wild boars on campus.

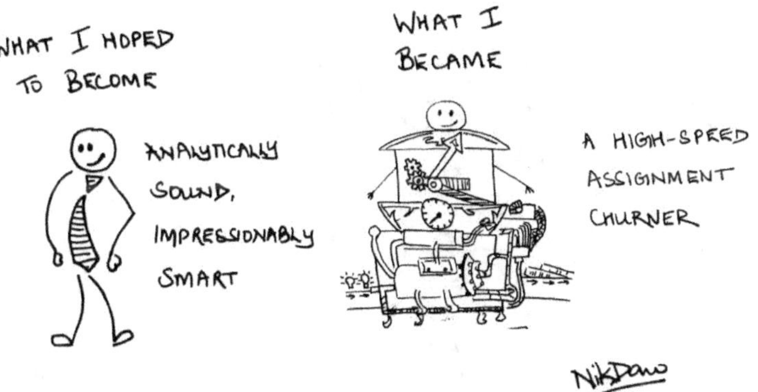

You win some, you lose some.

By Day

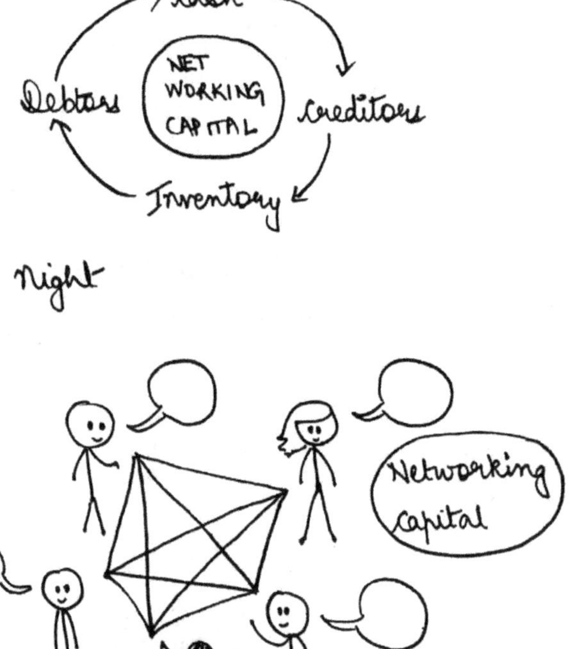

By Night

Networking soon turns into wriggling your bellies drunk.

Professor is teaching 'control limits' and a chart is displayed on the screen. Student tries to get too analytical about it. Prof: I think you're reading too much into it. If you stare at it any longer-you will see your mother's face in it.

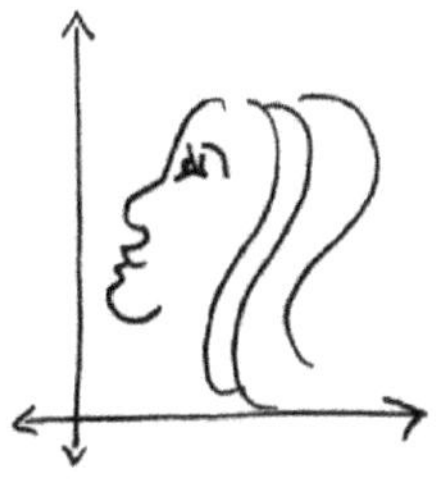

ACPE: Sir, with the lines between industries blurring, how do we define tech? When you say technology, what picture should I paint in my head? Prof: Depends on the size of your head.

Few days later...

Study group freeriding should be a non-bailable offence.

Abuse of Power

The path to embarrassment is easy.

no such thing as staying on top.

session 6

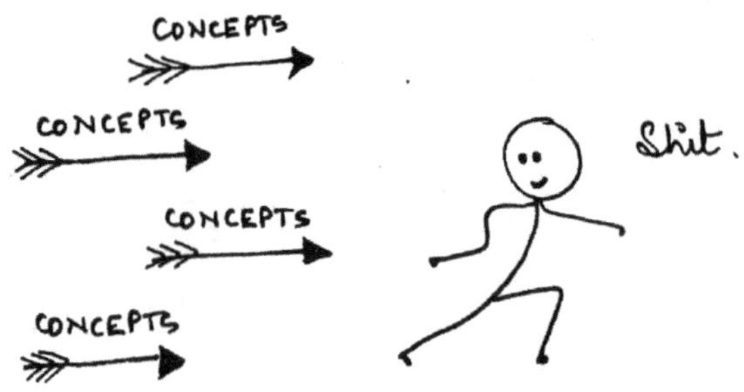

NikDaw

The bombarding never stops.

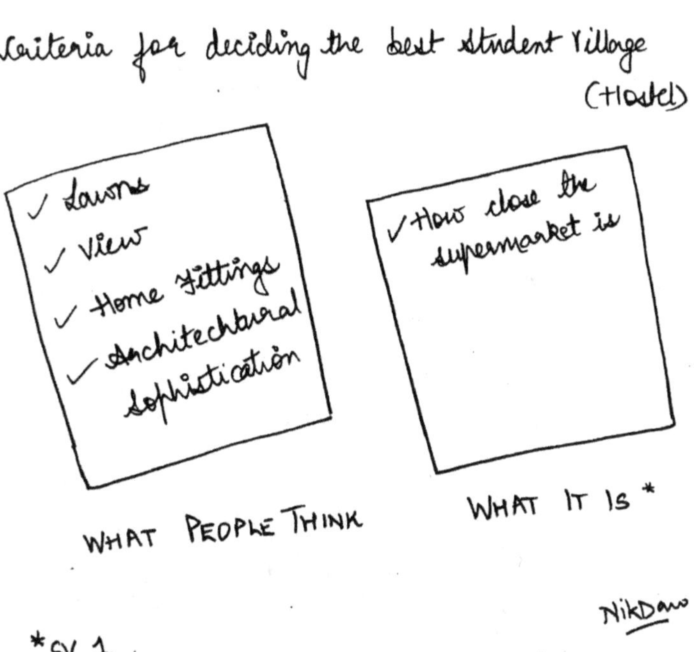

Being able to purchase a chocolate within minutes of feeling stress is a wonderful thing.

what I gather from class

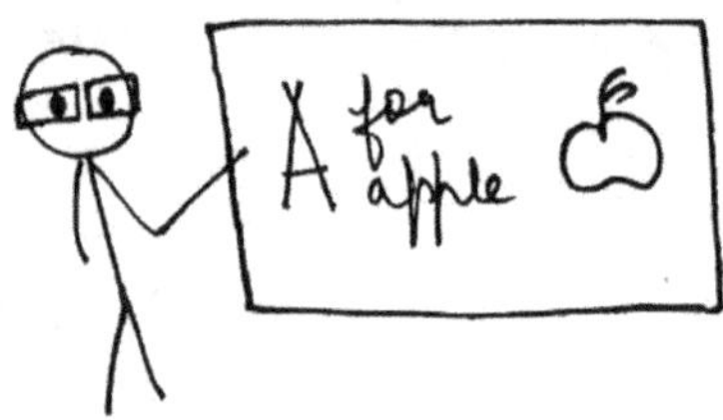

what comes in the exam

Q. In 2010, an apple's genome was sequenced as a part of which groundbreaking research?

NikDaw

Well played, Professor.

The transition is quick.

Classic Prisoner's Dilemma: We study hard to make it worse for ourselves.

There's always one guy whose class participation invokes these feelings

I'm sure you remembered that person right now.

The only thing that compares with MBA Jargon

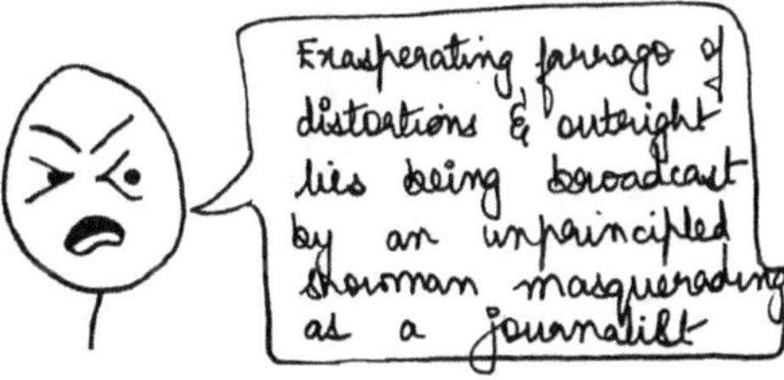

SHASHI THAROOR'S VOCABULARY

NikDaw

We study the "Surprising Robustness of the Self-Explicated Approach to Customer Preference Structure Measurement."

Loo Breaks between exams

What's worse than making eye contact between exams?
Honor code violations.

well done , Professor...

Have revised every
concept except XYZ.
Will understand
from someone later.

Quiz, next morning

NikDaw

Smiles in pain

A race for the best consulting jobs begins with the best CGPA.

Things you learn at B-school...

strong ~~written communication skills~~

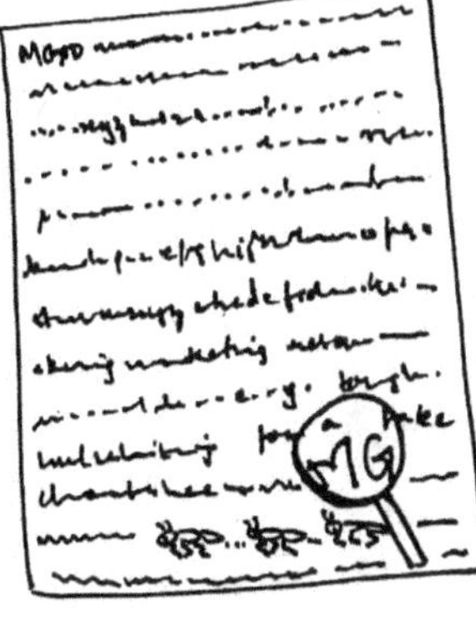

It's a handy skill for life. NOT.

(Un)Funny Bone

All for a few extra CP points.

Slave driving.

Team 1

Team 3

NikDaw

It's a victory in itself.

Bidding for courses

Indicative →

Actual →

NikDaw

We first indicate our intent for courses using a bidding system, which helps the school decide the demand for seats, and later place an actual bid for courses.

You're guaranteed to fear unemployment,
at some point.

Negotiations Noobs

First multi-group negotiation

NikDaw

*We took ourselves too seriously in negotiations'
role plays.*

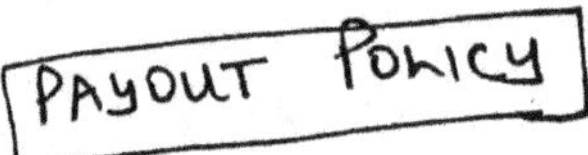

Modigliani and Miller were actually philosophers.

The truth about pre-placement talks..

"That's what they said".

Attending the course at 8am

Bidding is easy, waking is hard.

So not prepared to inter-woo.

While we attended to
Resume edits, cover letters, case paeps,
assignments

Lockdown feels.

Resume plans

NikDaw

Cashbacks always work, right?

What you make your resume sound like...

What you truly are...

Recruitments: Who wears the mask best?

Structure is everything.

Counter-Intuitive

(We get a limited number of counters for applying to job positions).

How to network effectively for jobs...

Also: 'Forward this resume to meet hot singles in your area'.

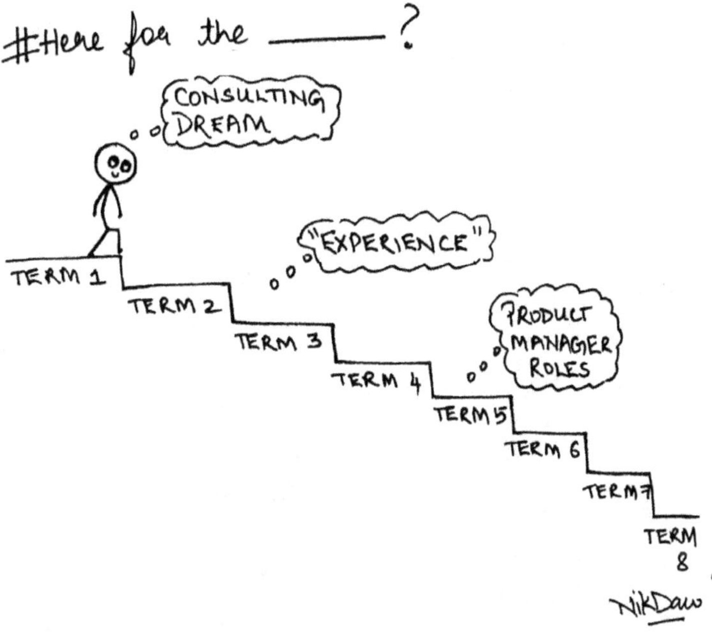

When the reality of the CGPA inadequacy hits you.

The MOST important question in recruitment

This question is a curse to all mankind.

A request for 'Champions' as well.

We are screened and weighed.

For the days are long, and full of terror.

The Pursuit of Happyness is endless.

The day after you get placed

It's a good sort of empty.

There's no stop button to the race.

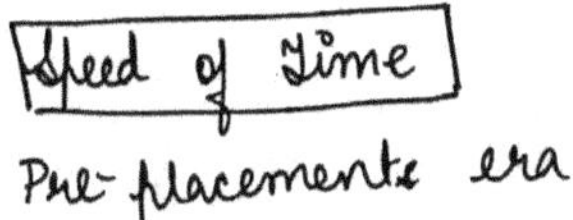

Pre-placements era

Post placements era

That helpless feeling.

Prof is making a table of pros and cons of each distribution chain on the board.

ACPE: BUT SIR...

Prof: (turns towards the class) I guess we'll have to stop writing to find out WHO WAS YELLING AT ME ???!

Prof: (explaining a scenario where there is no Nash equilibrium)

ACPE: (excitedly) Sir, in this case, there is no Nash equilibrium.

Prof: I think that should've been clear from the title of the slide.

You'll wrongly imagine the arbit class participation will someday stop.

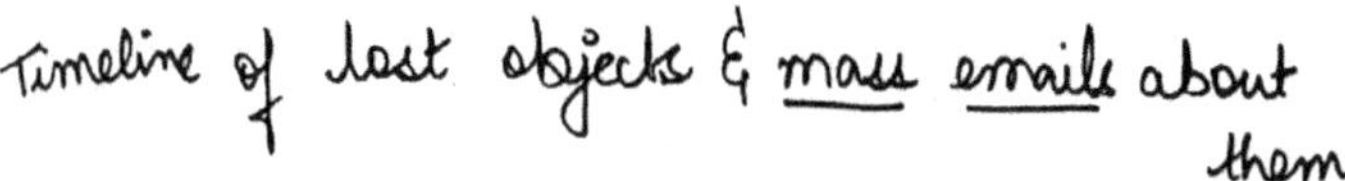

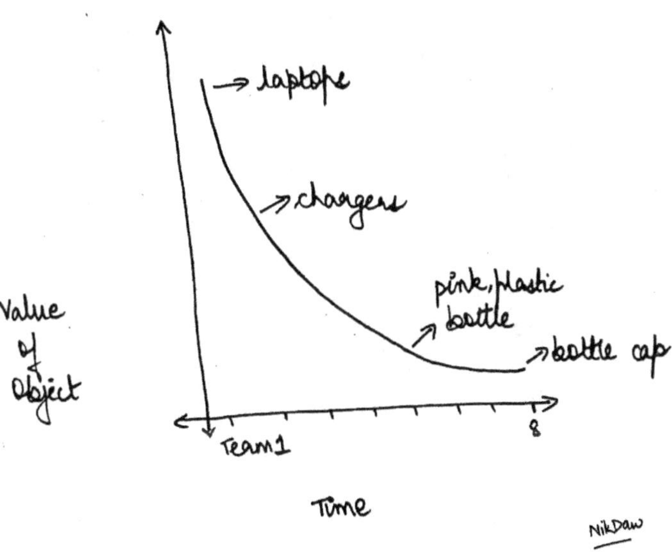

Beyond the realm of ridiculous.

They said you'll find love at Bschool

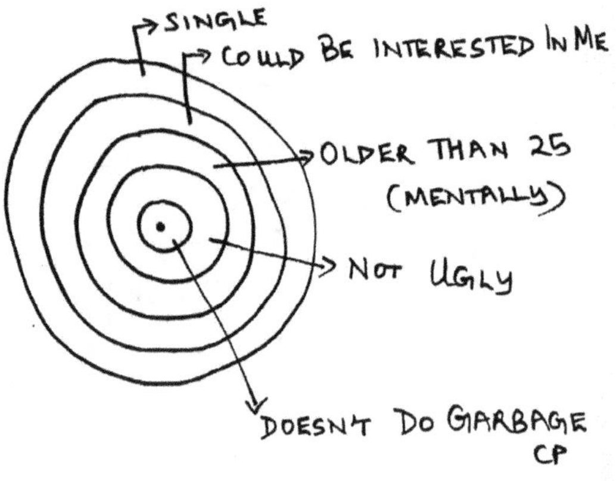

CP-CLASS PARTICIPATION

NikDan

Still not funny for some people.

Meta`prof´osis

NikDaw

We students aren't kind sometimes.

It's like everyone went for Vipassana

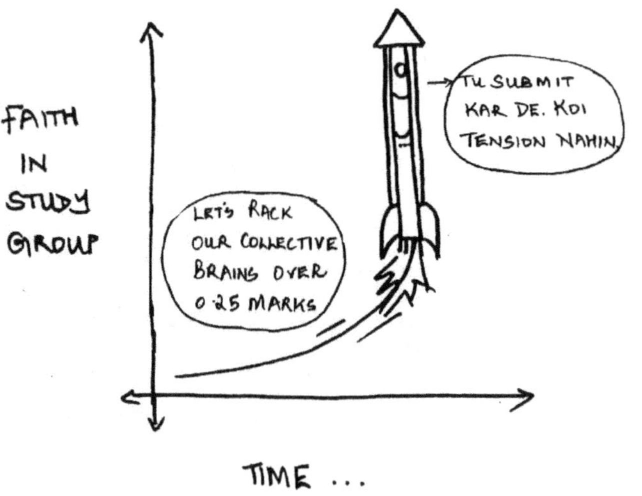

Several assignments start getting submitted, without as much as meeting group members.

Plans after checking the school gym

8 months later

Only so much you can do with your time at school.

what video conferencing is expected
to achieve

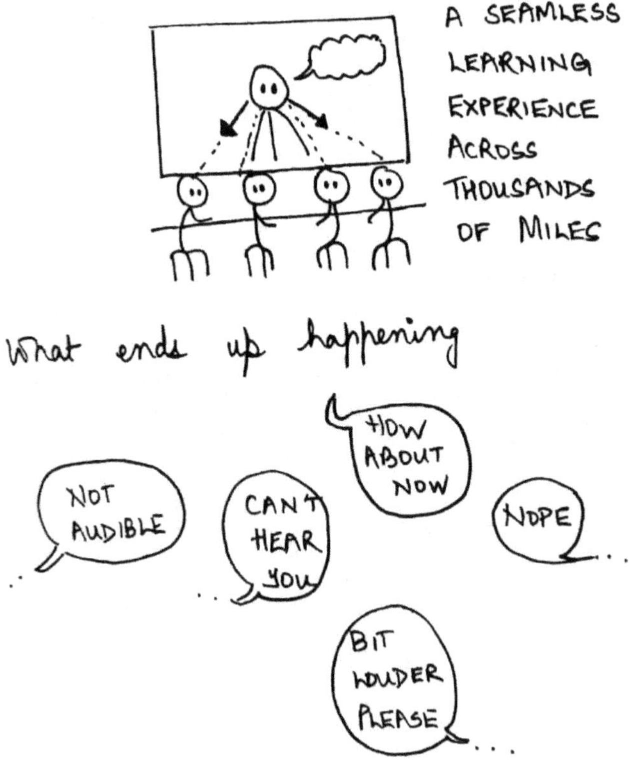

what ends up happening

"Technology, are you listening?"

You meet people. And then you meet their new selves.

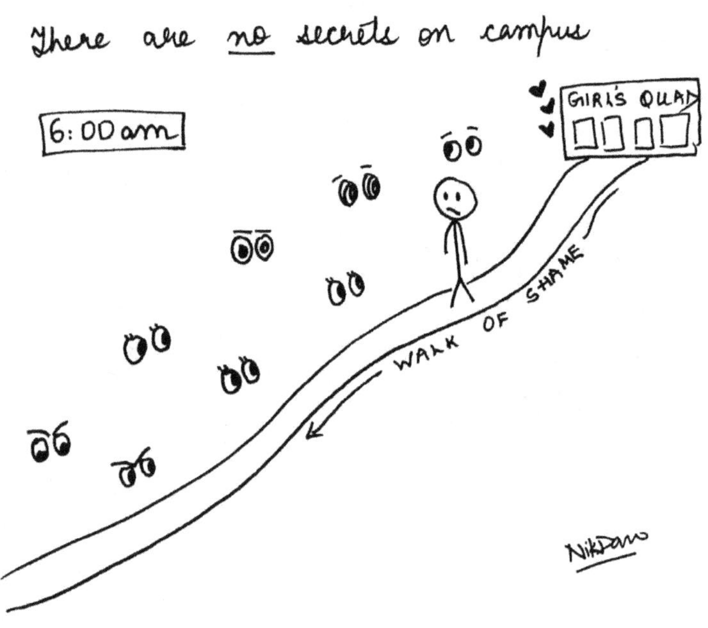

The campus brims with love birds.

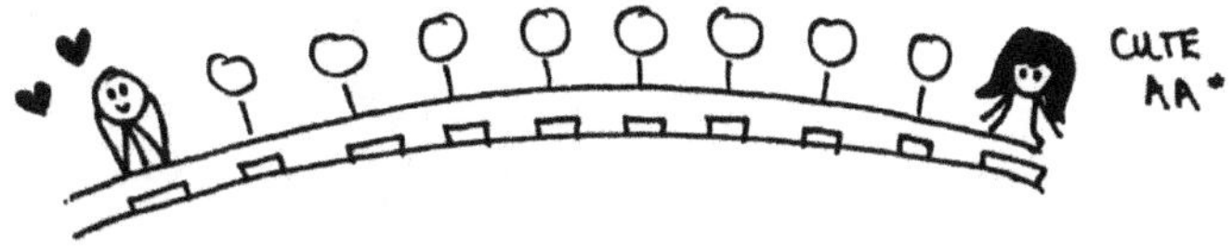

* ACADEMIC ASSOCIATE

NikDaw

"Usne waapis smile kiya, lagta hai patt gayi"
(She smiled back, think she's mine now).

Team 7, ladies and gentlemen

Sudden streak of rebelliousness.

Packing stuff usually takes half an hour

NOT ANY MORE

And then the trips from school begin!

MY RELATIONSHIP WITH CONJOINT ANALYSIS

SESSION 1

ALL ROSES AND BUTTERFLIES

SESSION 6

Forgive this simple child of God, O' Marketing!

Miscalculating the student loan principal is easy.

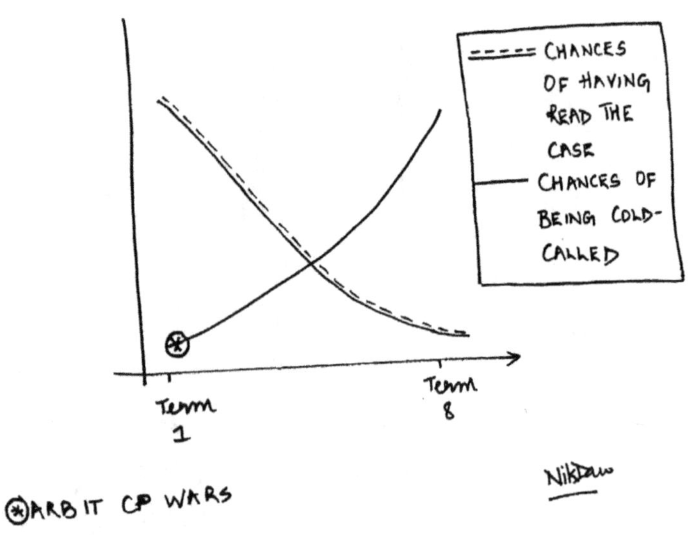

Profs play it smart, always.

we've come a long way

Team 1

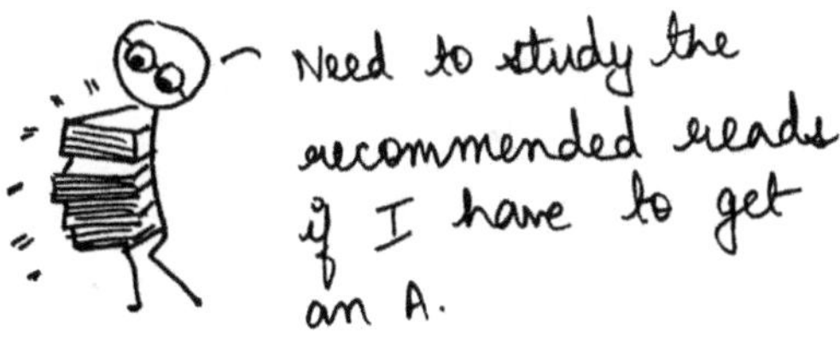

Team 8

NikDaw

The thing crawling in the lawns was not a snake. It was your friend.

Unbelievable inertia.

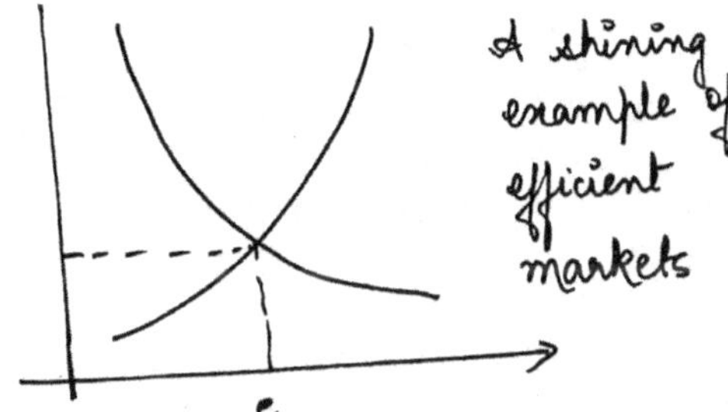

Thankfully, people learn from their bidding mistakes.

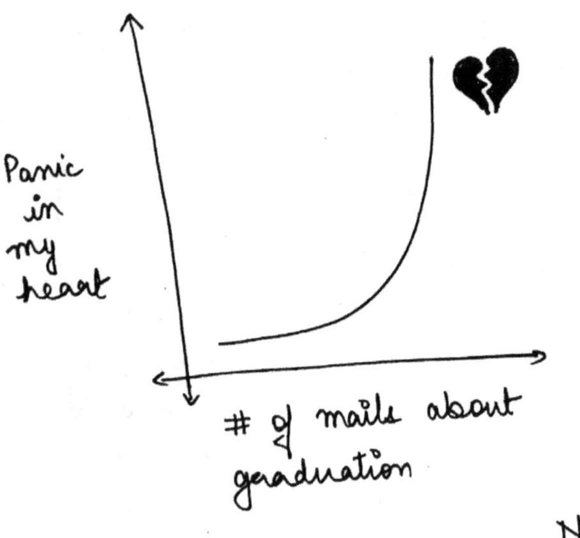

Cardiac arrests in Term 7.

Every now and then, you will still be amazed at what you don't know.

NikDaw

HAVE to let it sink.

Exit Graduation, Enter Debt Demon.

You are at a risk of forgetting 99% of what you learnt.

My favorite quote of all time.

Those were the best days of my life.

NikDono

Sigh

THE END

About the Author

Nikita Dawda

 Email   nikita.dawda11@gmail.com

 Instagram   https://www.instagram.com/nikdrawscomics/

 Facebook   https://www.facebook.com/Nikdrawscomics/

Nikita Dawda is a dual citizen of Mumbai and Bangalore. An MBA graduate from Indian School of Business, who found her way into the venture capital world and later in e-commerce with Flipkart and Meesho. Ever so often, she escapes the world of numbers through her comic page 'Nikdraws'. In her free time, she ponders over the perils of adulthood, while sipping a cup of tea, with a dreamy cat purring by her side.

Crowd-Funders

(names listed alphabetically)

Aakanksha Chhokra	DNV Kumara Guru
Aastha Shah	Gananath Misra
Abhash Kumar	Haripriyaa Murali
Abhishek Chaurasiya	Harish Chaudhary
Abhishek Ghag	Harish Dawda
Abhishek Kochhar	Harsh Gupta
Aditee Kale	Ishita Gupta
Aditya Verma	Jaimeen Bulsara
Akshat Arora	Jaskirat Kaur
Akshiv Baluja	Jeesha Jindal
Aman Sharma	Jyoti Senapati
Ameya Deshpande	Kanishka Verma
Amit Singh	Kapil Dawda
Anirudh Mathur	Karan Surana
Anirudh Rao	Kaustubh Maniar
Ankana D Rao	Khyati Kalra
Anupama Atmuri	Kiran Korma
Apoorv Chauhan	Konpal Agrawal
Aravind A N	Kriti B
Arth Shukla	Manasa Netrakanti
Arul Prakash	Manasa Surampudi
Arushi Sood	Matthew Dilip
Bharath Aitha	Megha Mathur

Mitalee M

Navjot Kaur

Nilayan Dey

Niranjan Yadav

Prabhakar Dwivedi

Prachi Gaur

Prachi Prachi Jha

Pranav Thakkar

Prashant Kumar

Prasooon Thapliyal

Prerana Agarwal

Raghav Behani

Rahuo Sethi

Richa Srivastava

Rishabh Jain

Rishabh Verma

Sai Tejaswini Y

Sameer Gujral

Sandeep Talla

Sehej Singh

Shivang Bhagat

Shobhana Raman

Siddharth Kataria

Simran Arora

Srikant Sree Ram

Srikar M

Srishti Mittal

Sudhanshu Pradhan

Swapnil Paroha

Swaroop Anand

Swaroopa Sanap

Tarun Firodiya

Tuhin Sharma

Utkarsh Garg

Utkrishta Kumar

Vaibhav Aggarwal

Vaibhav Chitrao

Vardhan Jain

Vineet Venugopal

Vinit Nalavadi

Zafar Hussain

Zoya Naqvi

μ

SURVIVING BUSINESS SCHOOL

A 'Nikdraws' Collection

Nikita Dawda

Email your questions, experiences,
and suggestions to the author at
nikita.dawda11@gmail.com

Your Experiences